V v

Victoria's Vacation and the Letter V

Alphabet Friends

by Cynthia Klingel and Robert B. Noyed

The
Child's
World®

Published in the United States of America by The Child's World®
P.O. Box 326
Chanhassen, MN 55317-0326
800-599-READ
www.childsworld.com

The Child's World®: Mary Berendes, Publishing Director

Editorial Directions, Inc.: E. Russell Primm, Editorial Director; Emily Dolbear, Line Editor; Ruth Martin, Editorial Assistant; Linda S. Koutris, Photo Researcher and Selector

Photographs ©: Thinkstock/Getty Images: Cover & 9; Photodisc/Getty Images: 10, 13; Corbis: 14, 17; Jonathan Blair/Corbis: 18; Emanuele Taroni/Photodisc/ Getty Images: 21.

Library of Congress Cataloging-in-Publication Data
Klingel, Cynthia Fitterer.
  Victoria's vacation and the letter V / by Cynthia Klingel and Robert B. Noyed.
    p. cm. — (Alphabet readers)
Summary: A simple story about a girl named Victoria and the things she and her mother do on vacation introduce the letter "v".
  ISBN 1-59296-112-6 (Library Bound : alk. paper)
[1. Vacations—Fiction. 2. Alphabet.] I. Noyed, Robert B., ill. II. Title. III. Series.
  PZ7.K6798Vi 2003
  [E]—dc21   2003006611

Note to parents and educators:
The first skill children acquire before becoming successful readers is individual letter recognition. The Alphabet Friends series has been created with the needs of young learners in mind. Each engaging book begins by showing the difference between the capital letter and the lowercase letter. In each of the books on the vowels and the consonants c and g, children are introduced to the different sounds that the letter can make. Finally, children see that the letters can be found at the beginning of a word, in the middle of a word, and in most cases, at the end of a word.

Following the introduction, children meet their Alphabet Friends. The friend in each story encounters many words that include the featured letter of that book. Each noun that begins with the title letter is highlighted in red with the initial letter of the word in bold. Above the word is a rebus drawing that establishes a strong picture cue.

At the end of each book, we have included three words lists. Can your young learners find all the words in each book with the title letter in them?

Let's learn about the letter **V.**

The letter **V** can look like this: **V.**

The letter **V** can also look like this: **v.**

The letter **v** can be at the beginning of a word, like volcano.

volcano

The letter **v** can be in the

middle of a word, like movie.

mo**v**ie

The English language doesn't have

any words that end in **v.**

Victoria and her mother are home on

vacation. **V**ictoria is very glad. They will

be home on **v**acation for five days.

The first day was over very fast. **V**ictoria

and her mother visited Grandma.

Victoria played the **v**iolin for Grandma.

"**V**ery good, **V**ictoria!" said Grandma.

Victoria was very busy on the second day.

She vacuumed every room for her mother.

Victoria also picked **v**iolets and put them

in a **v**ase.

On day three, **V**ictoria's mother looked

at the **v**egetables in the garden. It was

very weedy. **V**ictoria and her mother

weeded around the **v**egetables.

It was day four of **V**ictoria's **v**acation. It

was a play day. They played **v**olleyball

with **V**ictoria and her friends.

On the last day of **v**acation, **V**ictoria

and her mother visited the **v**ideo store.

They picked out a **v**ideo about a

volcano. It was very good!

Victoria and her mother had a great five

days of **v**acation. It's time for **V**ictoria to

go back to school.

Fun Facts

What do lettuce, broccoli, onions, carrots, potatoes, and peppers all have in common? They're all **v**egetables! **V**egetables are a certain type of plant grown to be used as food. But there is some confusion about which plants, or parts of plants, are truly **v**egetables. For example, a tomato is technically the fruit of the tomato plant. And peas are actually seeds. However, both tomatoes and peas are commonly considered **v**egetables.

A **v**olcano is an opening in Earth's surface through which lava, hot gases, ash, and rock pieces erupt. **V**olcanoes are often hills or mountains built around these openings from all the materials that have erupted. Most **v**olcanoes are underwater, but violent eruptions above sea level often have very serious consequences for humans. The most famous **v**olcano in history is Mount Vesuvius, in Italy. Almost 2,000 years ago it erupted, killing about 30,000 people and destroying three Roman cities, including Pompeii. Because the cities were covered in **v**olcanic ash, they were preserved through time and can now be studied.

To Read More

About the Letter V

Ballard, Peg. *Vets: The Sound of V.* Chanhassen, Minn.: The Child's World, 2000.

About Vegetables

Florian, Douglas. *Vegetable Garden.* San Diego: Harcourt Brace Jovanovich, 1991.

Lin, Grace. *The Ugly Vegetables.* Watertown, Mass.: Charlesbridge, 1999.

Tofts, Hannah, and Rupert Horrox (photographer). *I Eat Vegetables!.* New York: Zero to Ten Ltd., 1998.

About Volcanoes

Nirgiotis, Nicholas, and Michael Radecich (illustrator). *Volcanoes: Mountains that Blew Their Tops.* New York: Grosset and Dunlap, 1996.

Simon, Seymour. *Danger! Volcanoes.* New York: SeaStar Books, 2002.

Words with V

Words with V at the Beginning

vacation

vacuumed

vase

vegetables

very

Victoria

Victoria's

video

violets

violin

visited

volcano

volleyball

Words with V in the Middle

every

five

movie

over

About the Authors

Cynthia Klingel has worked as a high school English teacher and an elementary teacher. She is currently the curriculum director for a Minnesota school district. Cynthia Klingel lives with her family in Mankato, Minnesota.

Robert B. Noyed started his career as a newspaper reporter. Since then, he has worked in communications and public relations for a Minnesota school district for more than fourteen years. Robert B. Noyed lives with his family in Brooklyn Center, Minnesota.